Four Friends
IN
Summer

For Charles Massey
and his summer adventures—
and, of course, Mario
—T deP

SIMON & SCHUSTER BOOKS FOR YOUNG READERS
An imprint of Simon & Schuster Children's Publishing Division
1230 Avenue of the Americas, New York, New York 10020

Book design by Paula Winicur
The text for this book is set in Celestia Antiqua.
Manufactured in China

4 6 8 10 9 7 5 3

Library of Congress Cataloging-in-Publication Data
dePaola, Tomie.
Four friends in summer / written and illustrated by Tomie dePaola.—1st ed.
p. cm.
Summary: Four friends, Missy Cat, Mistress Pig, Master Dog, and Mister Frog, enjoy the warm and sunny days of
spring and summer together.
ISBN 978-0-689-85693-8 (hardcover)
[1. Spring—Fiction. 2. Summer—Fiction. 3. Friendship—Fiction. 4. Animals—Fiction.] I. Title.
PZ7.D439 Flg 2003
[E]—dc21
2002013324

Four Friends in Summer was previously published,
in different form, as the chapters entitled "Spring" and "Summer"
in *Four Stories for Four Seasons,* copyright © 1977 by Tomie dePaola
1116 SCP

Four Friends
IN
Summer

STORY AND PICTURES BY

TOMIE DEPAOLA

SIMON & SCHUSTER BOOKS FOR YOUNG READERS
New York London Toronto Sydney Singapore

ne fine day, Master Dog and Missy Cat decided to ask Mistress Pig and Mister Frog to join them in a stroll through the park.

"What lovely crocuses and daffodils," said Missy Cat.

"I like the tulips, too," said Master Dog.

"Nothing like a nice walk to make you feel chipper," said Mister Frog.

"Oh, look! An ice-cream stand," said Mistress Pig.

"I say," said Mister Frog, "how about a row around the lake?"

"Let's do it!" said Master Dog.

"I've never been rowing before," said Missy Cat.

"Oh, you'll love it, Kitty," said Mistress Pig.

"Oh, we sail the ocean blue," sang Mister Frog.

"My balloon," squealed Mistress Pig.

"Oh, dear," said Missy Cat.

"That's the first time *that's* ever happened," said Master Dog.

"So sorry," muttered Mister Frog.

"Are you all right, Kitty dear?" asked Mistress Pig.

"Rowing is so much fun!" said Missy Cat.

"When can we do it again?"

Since Missy Cat was the only one who wanted to go
rowing again, the four friends thought it would be fun to do
something they all enjoyed. They decided that each one would
plant a garden.

They all worked very hard as the summer went by.

"Now that summer's almost over, my friends," said Mister Frog, "I think we should visit each other's gardens."

"We can have a Garden-Viewing Day," said Missy Cat.

"Oh, goody," said Mistress Pig.

"Let's do it Thursday," said Master Dog.

The four friends agreed that Thursday would be a perfect day.

They all met at Missy Cat's garden.

"Pretty!" said Master Dog.

"Nothing like a well-planned flower garden,"
said Mister Frog.

"Those marigolds look good enough to eat,"
added Mistress Pig.

"Thank you, my dears," purred Missy Cat.

Next they went to Mister Frog's garden.

"Why, you have a water-lily and cattail garden,"
said Master Dog.

"So original!" said Missy Cat.

"You must tell me your secret," whispered Mistress Pig.

"The secret is water," answered Mister Frog.

"Does look rather nice, doesn't it?" he added.

Mistress Pig's garden was next.

"Oh, Piggy sweet, how practical," said Missy Cat.

"Never have I seen such pumpkins!" said Mister Frog.

"And those carrots. I love carrots," said Master Dog.

"I'm so pleased you like it," said Mistress Pig.

"Here, taste these tomatoes. They're delicious."

Finally they arrived at Master Dog's garden.

The three friends looked and looked.

"I say, Doggy—what happened?" asked Mister Frog.

"Poor Doggy, I'm *so* sorry for you," said Missy Cat.

"A *dirt* garden?" gasped Mistress Pig.

"You don't understand, dear friends," said Master Dog.
"It's a bone garden!"

The friends laughed and everyone agreed that there is no better way to enjoy a lovely day than strolling through a garden— no matter what kind of garden it is!